HILLS OF WILDFLOWERS

WHEN FLOWER REMEMBER US

PARAS RAI

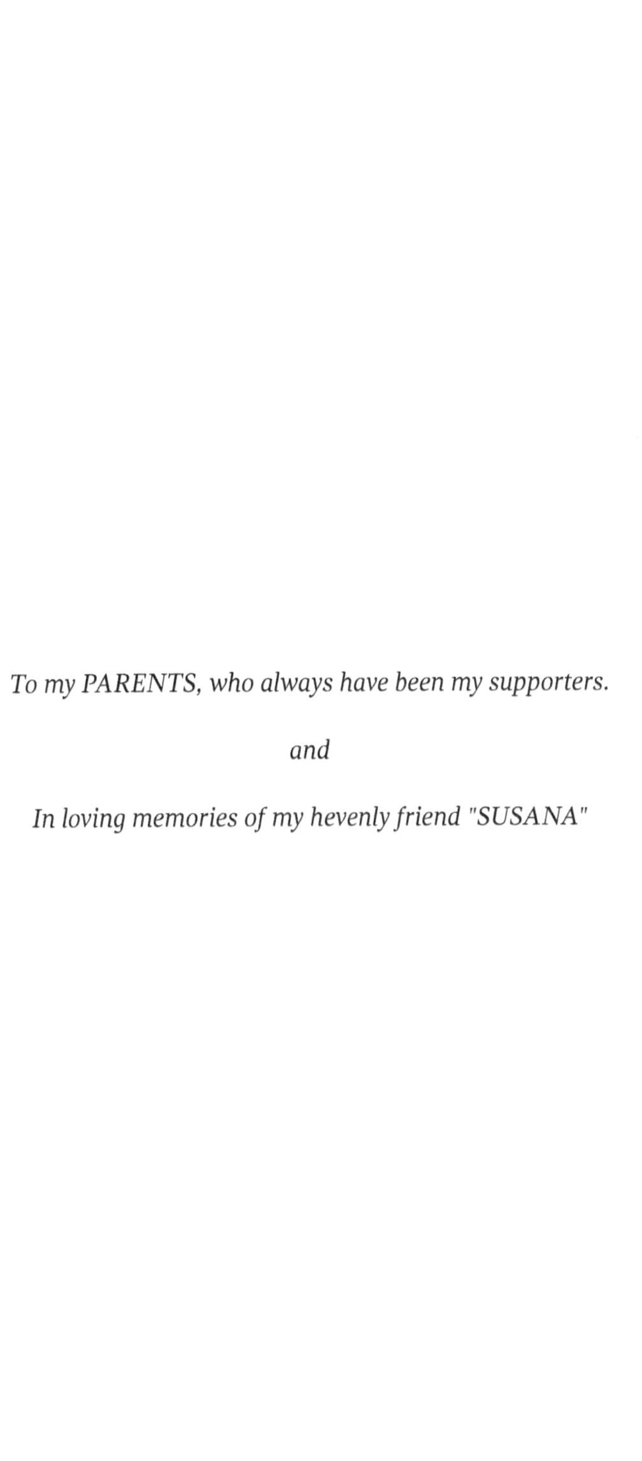

To my PARENTS, who always have been my supporters.

and

In loving memories of my hevenly friend "SUSANA"

Contents

Foreword

Some stories don' t begin with fireworks or dramatic confessions. Some stories begin with silence -unspoken glances, rainy school corridors, and a diary page that says more than a thousand words.

"HILLS OF WILDFLOWERS" is a story born from stillness. From the quite corners of the heart where one-sided love waits, hoping to become something more. It' s for everyone who ever loved in silence, who belived they weren' t enough yet loved fiercely anyway.

Laksh and Vedika are fragments of so many of us. This stroy breathes the air of easter hills, tastes like sunflower petels saved between pages. It' s not perfect - but it is real. And sometimes, real is all we need.

Thank You for picking up this book. I hope it makes you blush, ache, smile- and maybe, belive in the kind of love that waits, climbs, and writes its way into the clouds.

    - Paras Rai

Preface

This story began as a whisper- a quite idea scribbed in the margins of a notebook during lonely evenings and tender memories. It is not just about love, but about waiting. About how sometimes the people we quitely think of in crowded classroom or under starry skies are thinking of us too.

HILLS OF WILDFLOWERS is the journey of Laksh and Vedika- two hearts from the hills, caught in the slow dance of longing, timing, and silent promises. It's written with ink, but lived through petels, letters, old toy trains, and fleeting glances.

To everyone who' s ever loved without knowing if they were loved back - this one is for you.

Acknowledgements

This wouldn' t have been possible without the quite moments, the late- night thoughts, and the dreams i dared to pen down.

To my friends who listened patiently, gave honest feedback, and never laughed when i said, "I' m writing a love story" - i owe you more than words.

To my family - for the support, the space, and the belife, even when i doubted myself.

Finally to Vedika and Laksh.

Prologue

Before the first word was written,
     before a sunflower was ever pressed between pages,
     and before a quite boy looked up tp find a girl
     smling at nothing-
     there was silance.

Laksh

It was the first day of Class 11, and Laksh had taken his usual seat at the far end of the second row, next to the window. It gave him just the right excuse to look outside and not at people.

That was the day Vedika walked in.

She wore a maroon hoodie with the school badge half-tucked under her scarf, headphones still dangling around her neck. She had the kind of confidence Laksh could never fake—even when she looked lost, she owned the space like she belonged everywhere.

She plopped down on the seat next to him, dropped her books, and asked, "Hey, do you have an extra pen? Mine disappeared into some black hole."

Laksh slid one silently across the desk without looking up.

"Thanks, *window poet,*" she said casually.

He blinked. "What?"

"You look like the kind of guy who writes poems staring out at clouds."

He didn't reply, just gave the smallest smile and turned back to the window. That was the first time someone called him something more than just quiet.

Mid class 11

Vedika had become an inseparable part of the group by then—always joking, always the center of attention. But Laksh noticed something others didn't: whenever she laughed loudly, her eyes still searched for something.

One rainy day, when most of the school had stayed home, they ended up alone in the library. She found a doodle he had left on a loose paper—of a girl standing with a sunflower in one hand and mountains behind her.

"This looks like me," she said, showing it to him.

"It's just... someone."

"Uh-huh," she smirked. "So 'just someone' happens to wear the same earrings and hoodie as me?"

He didn't respond. She placed it in her diary.

Later that day, she told him with mock seriousness, "Laksh, if you ever write a poem about me, you better call me something cool.

He just nodded, too afraid to tell her it was already written, two pages deep in his secret diary.

Blue Umbrella

It was a Monday, and Darjeeling's unpredictable rain had turned the school courtyard into a mosaic of puddles and reflections. Most students had umbrellas—Laksh did not.

He stood near the corridor, watching the clouds burst open. And then came Vedika, spinning her blue umbrella like it was a dance partner.

"Hey window-poet," she grinned. "Need a lift?"

Laksh hesitated. "No, I'm fine. I'll wait."

"Oh come on," she said, grabbing his wrist. "You'll get soaked. And I'm not offering again."

That was the first time she touched him. Just the wrist, just a tug. But he felt it for the rest of the week.

They walked under her umbrella, shoulder to shoulder. His left side was completely drenched. She noticed.

"I thought you'd be smart enough to tilt it your way," she teased.

"I didn't want you to get wet," he replied, eyes still on the road.

She went quiet for a beat. "Stupid poet."

Later That Month

They started meeting on weekends. She'd come over with a bag of chips and say she was "bored of being popular." His mother adored her. His little sister once whispered, "Bhaiya, is she your *special friend?*"

He turned red. Vedika just laughed and ruffled the kid's hair.

They watched indie Nepali films, listened to Sufi songs she loved, and once spent a whole afternoon arguing whether charcoal or pencil sketching was more romantic.

"Charcoal is drama," Vedika said.

"Pencil is subtle. Like... love that's never said aloud."

"Ugh. You'd write a book called Subtle Suffering someday."

He smiled but didn't correct her. He had already started writing something in his diary. And the chapter title? Vedika.

Laksh

It was Teacher's Day. She had worn a green kurta, one earring missing, and a sunflower tucked behind her ear.

"I got this for you," she said casually, handing him a notebook.

Inside was a sticky note: For your poetry. Write about anything. Even about me, if you're brave enough.

He looked up at her. She winked.

That night, he wrote:

Dear Ved,

You gave me a sunflower today.

But you don't know you've been one to me all along—bright, impossible to ignore, and always looking at the sun.

And I? I'm the quiet hill you never see blooming behind you.

The half way confession

Board exams loomed like a mountain of dread, and most students buried themselves in coaching notes, sample papers, and revision timetables. But Laksh, true to form, found himself back in the art room every other evening, sketching flowers he couldn't name and poems he couldn't say out loud.

Ved hadn't stopped talking to him, but something had changed. Their conversations were shorter, less frequent. She didn't call him window poet anymore. He missed it more than he cared to admit.

One day after a mock test, Ved walked into the art room with a bottle of cold coffee and two samosas stuffed in a tissue. She plopped down beside him like she still belonged there.

"You still draw sad girls with wind in their hair?" she asked, peeking at his sketchbook.

Laksh smiled. "Not sad. Just... thinking."

Ved snorted. "Sure. Deep."

She looked at the drawing—another sketch of her, unintentionally maybe, standing under a tree filled with rhododendrons. This time, she held a sunflower in her hand.

"You really do like this flower, don't you?"

"Sunflowers follow the sun," Laksh said without thinking. "*They always know where the light is.*"

Ved looked down at her lap. "And what about rhododendrons?"

"They bloom even in high altitudes... stubborn and silent. You can't ignore them when they appear."

Her fingers tightened slightly on the cold coffee.

They sat quietly for a while. The silence between them wasn't awkward—but it was full.

Then Ved said, carefully casual, "Hey Laksh... If someone were to like you, I mean really like you... What would you do?"

He blinked. "What kind of question is that?"

"Just answer. Hypothetically."

He gave a dry chuckle. *"I'd say they're wasting their time. There are a hundred better options out there."*

Ved's laugh came a second too late. "Right. Of course."

She stood up, brushed samosa crumbs off her jeans. "Good talk, Mr. Humble."

He looked at her, unsure. "Was that... were you talking about—?"

She raised her hand like a stop sign. "Nope. Hypothetical. Just needed to check your ego."

She walked away, but this time—she didn't turn back to wink.

That night

Ved sat on her windowsill, watching mist swallow the moon. Her rhododendron plant sat quietly in the corner of the balcony, pink blooms leaning toward the dark.

She opened her diary.

Dear Laksh,

I joke because I'm scared.

I laugh because if I don't, I'll cry.

And I tease because I don't know how to say—

You make my heart quiet in the loudest way.

I wish you'd understand me like you understand rain, and poems, and flowers.

Yours, in case you ever notice,

Ved.

Flashback: Diwali Lights

Vedika arrived late to Laksh's place that Diwali. The sky was a firework in motion, and kids in the neighborhood were already burning sparklers and whirling chakris on the street.

Laksh stood at his gate, holding a half-burnt phooljhari and watching the crowd, when he spotted her—draped in a deep blue saree, a rhododendron pin in her hair, looking like she had stepped out of a festival song.

"Lost in lights, window-poet?" she teased.

"More like blinded," he muttered under his breath.

Behind her came Sujal, Vedika's cousin from Kalimpong—a lanky boy with too many opinions and an accent sharper than the cold air. And Anisha, Laksh's neighbor, a childhood friend who Ved never liked much but pretended to, because "girls have to be diplomatic, Laksh."

They lit diyas together. Sujal, with his endless chatter about college debates and politics. Anisha, stealing glances at Laksh when she thought no one noticed. Vedika, silently watching Laksh the whole time.

Later that night, while Sujal was off arguing with Anisha about capitalism and crackers.

"Ved" said Laksh, " *if you ever find me disappear check the summit of sandakphu. That's where my heart would go*".

But my feets won't help Laksh .

"Uff ho Ved, you're silly, take one vehicle"

They both laughed. Like they often does.

Ved whispered, "Can I tell you something?"

He turned, half-hoping.

"*I think the sky envies you,*" she said softly. "*It wants to write poetry like you.*"

Laksh laughed. "Nice try. Still not confessing, huh?"

Ved rolled her eyes. "Who says I haven't already?"

He blinked. "What?"

But just then, a rocket lit up the sky and the moment passed—like most moments between them did. Too loud to be heard, too

beautiful to be believed.

The draft

By the time the rhododendrons began to bloom in the hills again, something had changed.

Laksh noticed that Ved stopped waiting for him after classes. Their benches in tuition were still beside each other, but filled with books now—not glances. She'd started studying in the library more, mostly with Avik—the charming boy from the science section who knew too much about astrophysics and always carried chewing gum.

And yet... Ved still laughed at Laksh's jokes, still messaged him reels at midnight, still called him idiot poet when he spaced out. But there was a new tone to it. A slight distance. Like she was guarding herself.

Anisha noticed it too. "I think Ved likes you."

"She doesn't," Laksh said.

"She does," Anisha insisted. "And if you don't say something soon, someone else will."

One Morning

Ved was absent. And the next. And the next.

Laksh texted her.

Did your rhododendron wilt or what? Where are you, Ved?

No reply.

When she returned three days later, she looked fine. Smiled the same. Laughed the same.

But something in her had dimmed. She didn't tease anymore. Didn't call him names. She was quieter, less Ved, more... someone trying to forget.

That Evening – A Diary Entry

Laksh sat in his room, sketching a tea workers plucking the tea leaves.

Later he hold a pen instead and wrote

Dear Ved,

Did I miss the moment?

Were you trying to tell me something all along, and I thought it was just a joke?

I wish I could go back to that Diwali night.

Maybe I'd ask you again.

Maybe I'd listen better.

Meanwhile – Ved's Phone Notes

Laksh,

You never really saw me, did you?

I wanted to be your story.

But I think I became just your muse.

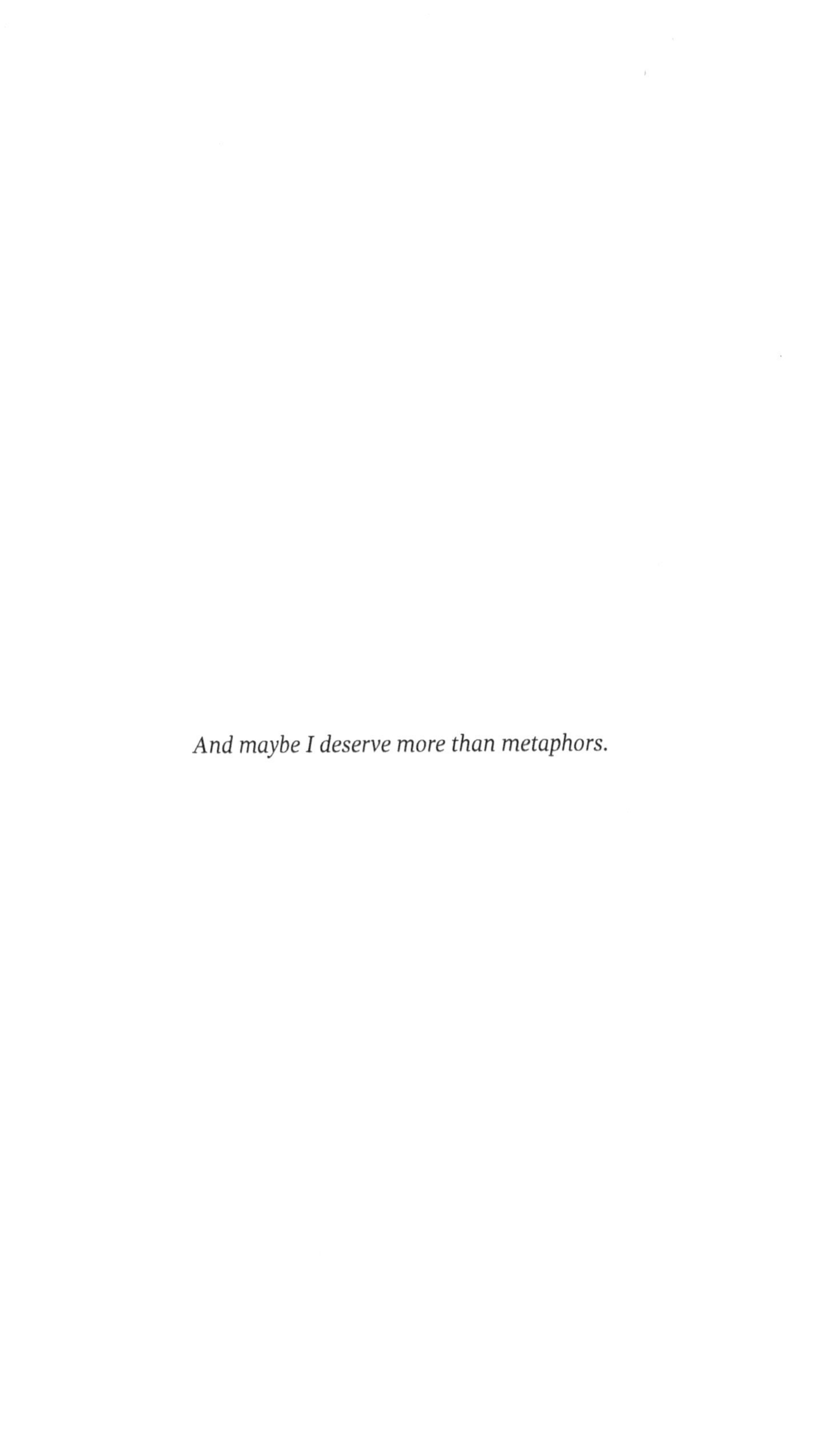

And maybe I deserve more than metaphors.

Boards

The morning of the English board exam was colder than usual. The kind of cold that doesn't just numb your fingers—it wraps around your chest and stays there.

Laksh reached school early, his admit card folded neatly inside his old canvas file. He sat alone on the steps outside the exam hall, trying to revise Macbeth but ending up staring at the trees swaying in the distance.

A voice broke through. "You'll fail Shakespeare if you keep watching trees like that."

He turned. *Ved.*

She wore a grey cardigan over her kurti, hair tied back messily, a red tikka on her forehead. It was the first time in weeks she had spoken to him without a group or a script.

Laksh smiled weakly. "I've been revising. In my head."

Ved sat beside him, cross-legged like always.

There was silence, but not the awkward kind. It was filled with a thousand memories. A thousand almost-confessions. The Diwali night. The tea breaks. The endless tuition evenings. The notebook poems. The time he gave her a pencil skctch of a girl under rhododendron trees and she smiled for too long.

And then—she handed him something.

A pen.

Black. Smooth. Simple.

"My lucky pen," she said.

"I can't take this," Laksh whispered.

"You'll write better poems with it," she replied, eyes on the sky.

He took it with a half smile, his fingers brushing hers for just a second longer than they should have. *"Thank you... Vedika."*

She flinched.

Not because of his voice. But because he said her real name. Not Ved, not anything else.

Just Vedika.

And something in that broke her a little.

During the Exam

Laksh couldn't focus. Every word on the paper looked like her handwriting. Every poem reminded him of her laugh.

A 10-marker question asked: "Discuss a moment of emotional transformation in any character from the texts."

He stared at it.

And wrote:

It was not Macbeth or Portia who changed. It was me.

I changed when I realized that someone can love you silently,

Deeply, in jokes and stolen glances, and late-night texts.

I changed when I lost the moment to say—

I love you too, Ved. Maybe always did.

He stopped, blinked. Then erased the last line, just leaving the first part of the answer and finished the rest of the paper like a normal student.

After the Exam

Students gathered outside, comparing answers. Ved was surrounded by her usual gang—Sujal, Avik, Anisha. She laughed with them. But her eyes scanned the crowd, looking for Laksh.

He wasn't there.

He had left early. Without saying a word.

And yet—when she opened her exam booklet later (the school let them view copies post-evaluation)—she found something scribbled lightly under his roll number:

"For the girl who gave me her lucky pen.

I hope she knows she's been my luck all along."

She smiled. A soft, bitter, proud smile.

Laksh diary

Dear Ved,

You were never just a side character in my story.

You were the ink.

I wish I had told you that under the rhododendron tree, or when we sat beside that old hill, or during the Diwali night.

But maybe love doesn't always arrive with trumpets.

Sometimes, it waits in a borrowed pen.

Sometimes, in a skipped goodbye.

POST BOARDS

The exams were finally over.

Notebooks were thrown in the air, halls emptied of stress, and group photos taken with too much laughter and too little sincerity.

And yet, amidst all the joy, Ved felt hollow.

She looked for Laksh among the crowd. He wasn't there. Again.

She waited near the school gate. Nothing.

She checked her phone—no messages. Not even a meme.

That Night

Ved sat on her bed, eyes scanning the stars from her window. Anisha was on call, talking about what everyone was doing post-exams. Sujal had planned a road trip. Avik was applying to Delhi. Everyone was scattering.

"I think... I might leave, Ani," Ved said quietly.

"What?"

"Mum got transferred to Gangtok. She wants me to come. New start, new college. It's all happening so fast."

Anisha was silent.

"I want to tell him," Ved whispered.

"Then tell him."

Ved smiled faintly. "Yeah. I will."

The Next Morning

She woke up early, wore his favorite color—mustard yellow—and tucked a rhododendron in her braid.

She even wore the sunflower pendant he gifted her during Secret Santa, the one he bought thinking it was a keychain and then blushed for hours when she wore it around her neck.

She reached his home.

The gate was locked.

She called.

Switched off.

She messaged.

"Hey. I need to see you today. Important."

No reply

Then a text from Anisha pinged:

"He left this morning. Trekking. Sandakphu."

Her heart dropped.

"Gone?"

"Yeah. Said he needed air."

A Week Before

Laksh to his diary:

I want to go where the air is thin and my thoughts don't echo so loud.

I want to write her name on a hilltop and leave it to the winds.

Maybe it's better this way—*if she's moving on, I should too.*

She deserves the sky. And I've only ever offered clouds.

Vedika

She walked back home slowly. Past the tea stall they always met at. Past the bookstore where she caught him reading poetry with shaky fingers. Past the place he once whispered, "You make winters feel like spring."

When she got home, she wrote him a letter.

But she never sent it.

Dear Laksh,

You always waited for a sign.

A sign that I loved you.

I gave it—in the way I laughed at your worst jokes,

In the way I noticed your silences louder than your words,

In the way I held that pen out like it was more than ink.

I'm leaving.

I wanted to say it to your face,

But you're gone again...

Like always.

I hope Sandakphu heals you.

And if you find a sunflower there,

Think of me under the rhododendron trees.

Love,

Ved

(Your Infinity, always.)

She folded it. Kept it inside the poetry book he once borrowed. And cried—not the dramatic kind, but the quiet sobs that taste like everything unsaid.

sandakphu

Laksh sat under a tree, the same one from his first solo trek.

He took out his diary.

And wrote:

Dear Ved,

I missed the moment again, didn't I?

I wish I had stayed.

I wish I had said it.

I love you.

More than metaphors.

More than mountains.

More than the idea of being good enough for you.

Come find me, if you ever can.

Or wait.

And I'll find you.

If you ever remember

I'll be waiting for you on the summit.

A soft wind passed through the hills of Sandakphu. A rhododendron petal floated down beside him. He picked it up, held it against the sky.

It looked like her smile.

Summit

It was 6:45 a.m. when Laksh reached the summit.

The clouds below him moved like a slow orchestra, and the wind carried whispers that almost sounded like her name. He sat on a flat rock near the edge, the rhododendrons swaying around him like a quiet audience. In his hands was a single sunflower, wrapped in newspaper.

His fingers were freezing, but he held the flower as If it were breathing.

He was waiting.

He had been waiting since sunrise.

Laksh had left for this trek hoping to lose her memory somewhere between the ridges and pine forests. But all it had done was bring her closer—her laugh echoing in the breeze, her face floating in the clouds, her absence louder than any mountain silence.

And now... he was here.

At the place he had once joked about.

"If I ever disappear, you'll find me at the summit of Sandakphu."

He never thought she'd remember that.

Vedika: two days earlier

Vedika's room was in chaos.

Her mother stood by the door with packed bags. "We're leaving tomorrow morning, Vedika. Your father wants us in Gangtok by Monday."

She stood there, frozen. "Tomorrow?"

"There's nothing left here for you anymore," her mother said softly. "Board exams are over. Let's go. You'll thank me later."

Vedika didn't respond.

Later that evening, with her hands trembling and eyes swollen from holding back everything she didn't say, she walked down to Laksh's home. The lights were off except for the tiny bulb outside.

His grandmother opened the door, recognizing her instantly. "Laksh's not home, beta. He left for Sandakphu yesterday."

"I... I know," she replied

She pulled an envelope from her pocket, slightly damp from her palm.

"Can you give this to him when he comes back?"

The old woman nodded gently, as if she already knew the weight of unsent words.

Vedika smiled a goodbye and walked away.

Back at the Summit

Laksh waited till the fog became a blanket.

By 10:30 a.m., he knew.

She wasn't coming.

But still, he stayed a little longer.

He sat there with the sunflower beside him, scribbling quietly in his diary:

Dear Vedika,

You once asked me why I love sunflowers. Because they always turn to the light—even when the sky looks like it's falling apart.

Today I waited for you like that.

Like a sunflower staring at a storm.

And I think... I'll keep waiting. Even if you're in Gangtok now. Even if the clouds never clear.

With love,

Laksh.

Grandma

Vedika

Meanwhile, in a car speeding past Kalimpong.

Vedika stared out the window, biting her lip to keep the tears from falling.

In her hand was a rhododendron—pressed, but not perfect.

"I hope you waited," she whispered to the sky,

"Because I did too. Just in a different place."

Laksh

After days of climbing, cold wind, and lonely skies, Laksh finally returns home.

His shoes are muddy. His heart? Worse.

He's not expecting anything—except maybe the comfort of his room. But as he enters, his grandmother hands him a folded letter wrapped in a piece of white cloth.

"There's something for you," she says quietly.

Inside: a dried rhododendron, a few sunflower petals, and a folded piece of paper written in her unmistakable handwriting.

It smells faintly of the lavender perfume Vedika always wore during exams.

His hands hesitate. Then, slowly, he unfolds it.

Vedika's Letter

(Written two nights before she left for Gangtok)

"Window Poet ~"

You once told me you write best when the wind slips through your window.

So today I sat beside mine, and for once, tried to understand you.

Tried to feel what it meant to carry a thousand words in silence,

And bury a thousand more behind a smile.

I'm leaving, Laksh.

Gangtok is calling like some cruel echo,

And this time I can't ignore it.

I wanted to meet you at the summit. I swear I did.

I even packed an extra jacket—your favorite color, remember?

I even learned the map.

But the world has its own plans. And my mother had tickets.

So I leave behind this letter.

And my love.

And all the things I never said properly because I was too busy making it sound like a joke.

I love you, Laksh.

Not the "from the movies" kind.

But the kind that notices how you blink three times when nervous.

The kind that saved every poem you ever wrote, even the torn ones.

*The kind that waited in silence, hoping you'd just once say "Ved"
without laughing.*

You did.

And I smiled like a child given the sky.

You may never reply to this.

*You may tear it, or tuck it in the back of that sunflower-filled diary
you call a heart.*

But I had to say it, once.

If this is goodbye... then thank you.

For letting me fall without fear.

For being my poetry when I ran out of words.

For making even silence feel sacred.

One day, I hope the sky takes you somewhere beautiful.

*And if I'm lucky, maybe you'll remember me when the wind sneaks
through your window.*

With all the courage I could gather,

Vedika

(Your Ved—just this once)

He reads it once.

Then again.

Then once more, aloud, like reading it might bring her voice into the room.

And then he does something he hasn't done in years.

He cries.

Not the quiet kind—but the messy, breathless kind, as if the letter reached into him and broke something open.

He clutches the petals like they were still warm from her hands.

———————

The morning after returning from the trek, Laksh barely slept. His pillow smelled faintly of rhododendron, and the letter kept replaying in his mind like a forgotten melody suddenly remembered.

His grandmother, silent most of the day, watched him over the rim of her teacup.

"You should go," she finally said.

He looked up, dazed. "Go where?"

"To her. To Gangtok."

He blinked.

She nodded toward the letter still folded carefully beside the small lamp on the table. "You think love waits around in alleys or behind old trees? No, beta. Love waits in people. If she's yours, even the Himalayas can't keep her away. But you must go."

Laksh didn't reply. He just nodded, slowly, and that evening, packed a small bag again—less clothes, more courage.

Before he left, his grandmother placed something in his hand.

The small, fragile flower he had carried all the way from Sandakphu.

The one he had meant to give her if she had met him at the summit.

The sunflower. Dry now, but still golden like a stubborn memory.

MG Marg, Gangtok

The streets of MG Marg were dressed for tourists—soft prayer flags fluttering above, distant laughter, echoes of cafés and camera clicks. But for Laksh, everything was a blur.

He stood in the middle of the square, holding the sunflower wrapped in old newspaper. He didn't bring his phone. Didn't text her.

He just waited.

At one point, he sat on a bench across from a bookstore they both used to dream about visiting. He even smiled at the name—"Rachna Books." She had once said it sounded like a secret recipe.

People passed. Old men. Couples. School kids. A street musician played a Nepali flute that made his heart ache harder.

And then—

She appeared.

Not like a movie. Not in slow motion.

She was just there. Standing at the edge of the street, wearing a peach-colored shawl, hair tied in a loose bun, hands tucked nervously in her jacket.

He didn't move at first.

She saw him. And smiled.

Not the loud kind. The soft kind that only two people in the world would understand.

He stood up, walked to her, and didn't say a word.

Instead, he handed her the sunflower.

Her hands shook a little as she took it.

"It's from the summit," he whispered.

"I know," she said.

There was a pause.

"I thought you'd be mad," she murmured.

"I was," he said. "Then I read the letter again."

Vedika smiled, eyes glistening. "So... what now?"

He looked at her, then at the sky.

"Now," he said softly, "we stop writing letters. And start talking."

And just like that—no music, no dramatic kiss, no fireworks—just two people standing on MG Marg, holding a dried flower like it was the rarest thing on Earth.

———————

The air in Gangtok was cooler by evening. The clouds hung low, brushing past rooftops like an old friend. After MG Marg's quiet reunion, neither Laksh nor Vedika said much. But it wasn't the kind of silence that needed fixing—it was the kind that tasted like warmth.

"Come," she said, brushing her shoulder gently against his, "there's a café just around the bend. You'll like it."

They walked side by side, occasionally bumping into each other, like two school kids too shy to hold hands.

The café was tucked between a travel agency and an art store. The kind of place that smelled like cinnamon and memories. Wind chimes at the door, wooden chairs, yellow lamps. A sleepy cat on the window ledge.

They sat in a corner booth, away from the door. She ordered ginger lemon tea for both, and when the waiter left, Laksh looked at her with a mock frown.

"Still drinking this sad herbal mess?"

She smirked. "Still writing sad boy letters in the rain?"

Touché.

Laksh blinked. "You read that one?"

"Of course I did," Vedika said, crossing her arms. "You left it open on your desk one day in class. The one that started with 'Let me sit alone for a while.'" She mocked his tone. "So dramatic, Laksh."

He groaned and hid his face in the menu.

She laughed—a quiet, belly-deep laugh that made his chest bloom.

"I didn't mean for anyone to read that," he mumbled.

"I know," she said, sipping her tea. "That's why I read it twice."

He peeked up, smirking. "Stalker."

"Poet."

"Troublemaker."

"Lover boy."

He choked on his tea. "Excuse me?!"

She shrugged, eyes playful. "I mean... you did walk around Sandakphu carrying a sunflower. Alone. For a girl. Who didn't even show up."

Laksh looked away dramatically. "She stood me up."

Vedika leaned in, teasing. "She also wrote you a four-page letter with flower petals and a poem that started with window poet~. So maybe cut her some slack."

He met her eyes. And neither of them looked away.

There was a soft pause.

He whispered, "You remembered that poem?"

She nodded. "I never forgot."

They spent over two hours in that café. Talking. Laughing. Avoiding eye contact when the conversation drifted too close to what now.

But just as they were leaving, Vedika reached out and touched the sleeve of his jacket.

"Hey... Laksh?"

"Hmm?"

"I'm sorry."

"For what?"

"For not coming to the summit. For Gangtok. For all of it."

He smiled, just a little. "You're here now."

And she smiled back.

"Yeah. And you're still annoying."

He chuckled. *"You're still Infinity in my diary."*

She raised her eyebrows. "Still? Even after all this?"

He nodded slowly, eyes soft.

"You'll always be more than I can ever put into words."

And this time, she blushed.

SUMMIT

Two years later

The cold hadn't changed in Sandakphu. The wind still whispered in rhododendron groves. The sky still knew how to blush at dawn.

But something had changed in Laksh.

He stood near the same bend where he once waited with a sunflower. But this time, he wasn't alone.

Vedika was beside him—wrapped in a deep maroon shawl, cheeks red from the cold, her hand quietly folded into his.

No letters this time. No unfinished confessions.

Just presence.

"Remember this place?" he asked, pointing toward a distant peak.

She smiled. "Of course. This is where I didn't show up."

He laughed. "Yeah. And this is where I waited like a lovesick poet"

They stood in silence again, watching the valley below. He squeezed her hand gently.

"I still write, you know."

She looked at him. "About me?"

"Only ever about you."

She blushed—still the same way she did when he first said her name aloud. "Do you still call me...?"

"Infinity? No."

She looked up, surprised.

He shrugged, looking at her with a soft kind of affection. "I don't need to anymore. You're not an unreachable sky now. You're here. With me."

That made her eyes mist a little. "So what do you call me now?"

He leaned in, touched his forehead gently to hers, and whispered,

"Vedika."

Just Vedika. And somehow, it felt more sacred than any poem.

They stayed a while longer at the summit, laughing, sharing snacks, taking blurry photos. Just like every other couple—but also nothing like any other couple.

Because between them lived not just a love,

But letters,

Waiting rooms,

Unshared benches,

Train announcements,

Lost flowers,

Found flowers,

Missed moments,

And moments that never missed.

— — — —

When it was time to descend, Vedika looked at him and said, "We're still going to be a little apart after this, right?"

He nodded. "College. Work. Life."

She paused. "That okay with you?"

He smiled, reached into his bag, and pulled out a pressed sunflower—the same one from two years ago, now kept between pages of his diary.

"I kept this for the days you weren't around."

Her eyes widened.

"And this," he added, pulling a tiny rhododendron bloom she'd once tucked behind her ear, "for the days I missed your smile."

Vedika couldn't speak for a while. She only leaned in, hugged him tighter than ever before, and whispered,

"I'll always be the girl who wanted to climb the mountain with you."

He replied,

"And I'll always be the boy who saved the flowers."

Laksh

Postscript on Laksh diary:

She still laughs like sunshine. And I still write when I miss her. But now, she reads them sitting next to me.

Now,

Ved is no longer fiction, she is infinity.

About The Author

Paras Rai hails from gorubathan, a quite, beautiful town nestled in the kalimpong district of West Bengal. A place where clouds often kiss the hills and stories float in the mist, it' s where Paras found not just his inspiration- but also his voice.

Author' S Note

I never thought this story would leave my notebook. But somewhere between unspoken love and a trek through the clouds, *Hills of wildflowers* found its wings.

This book is not just fiction - it' s a piece of my heart.

Thank You for holding it in your hands.

With all my love,

-- *Paras*